Quick as a Wink, Fairy Pink

Lesley Gibbes & Sara Acton

working **t**itle **p**ress
An imprint of HarperCollins*Children's Books*

For Rodney, Austin & Georgia
With special thanks to Jane Covernton,
Sara Acton and Margaret Connolly – L.G.

For Polly – S.A.

Working Title Press
An imprint of HarperCollins*Children'sBooks*, Australia

First published in Australia in 2016
by Publishing Design Studio Pty Ltd
This edition published in 2018
by HarperCollins*Publishers* Australia Pty Limited
ABN 36 009 913 517
harpercollins.com.au

For Lucy W, who wanted a 'fairy' book

HarperCollins*Publishers*
Level 13, 201 Elizabeth Street, Sydney NSW 2000, Australia
Unit D1, 63 Apollo Drive, Rosedale, Auckland 0632, New Zealand

A catalogue record for this book is available from the National Library of Australia

ISBN: 978 1 9215 0487 7 (paperback)

Designed and set in Clarendon Light by Liz Nicholson, design BITE
Sara Acton used watercolour, ink and collage for the illustrations in this book
Colour reproduction by Graphic Print Group, Adelaide
Printed and bound in China by RR Donnelley on 128gsm Matt Art

51 50 49 48   17 18 19 20

Five little flutter fairies going off to bed,

Fairy Blue, Fairy Green, Fairy Gold and Red.

But one of them is hiding. Which fairy do you think?

Could it be the smallest one?

YES!

It's Fairy Pink.

Fairy Blue is brushing her teeth.

Fairy brush, fairy paste, fairy teeth so white.

Fairy floss, fairy rinse, fairy smile so bright.

'Now my teeth shine like new.

It's time for bed,' says Fairy Blue.

But someone's playing hide and seek.

Can you see her? Take a peek.

Quick as a wink, find Fairy Pink!

Fairy Green is having a bath.

Fairy soap, fairy sponge,

fairy fill the tub.

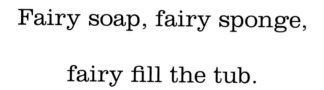

Fairy splish, fairy splash,

fairy rinse and scrub.

'I'm washed and dried and squeaky clean.

It's time for bed,' says Fairy Green.

But someone's playing hide and seek.

Can you see her? Take a peek.

Quick as a wink, find Fairy Pink!

Fairy Gold is

dressing for bed.

Fairy top, fairy pants, fairy twist and twirl.

Fairy hat, fairy scarf, fairy spin and whirl.

'I'm nice and warm. I won't get cold.'

'It's time for bed,' says Fairy Gold.

But someone's playing hide and seek.

Can you see her? Take a peek.

Quick as a wink, find Fairy Pink!

Fairy Red is reading a book.

Fairy tale, fairy rhyme,

fairy laugh and giggle.

Fairy chant, fairy song,

fairy clap and wriggle.

No more stories, sleepy head.

'It's time for bed,' says Fairy Red.

But someone's playing hide and seek.

Can you see her? Take a peek.

Quick as a wink, find Fairy Pink!

PEEK-A-BOO! We found you!

Fairy Pink is going to bed.

Fairy tired, fairy yawn, fairy goodnight hug.

Fairy bed, fairy soft, fairy warm and snug.

Pull up the sheets, quick as a wink.

'I'll blow you a kiss,' says Fairy Pink.

Five little flutter fairies tucked up tight in bed,

Fairy Blue, Fairy Green, Fairy Gold and Red.

But one of them is fast asleep. Which fairy do you think?

Could it be the smallest one?

YES!

It's Fairy Pink.